POOH INVENTS
A NEW GAME

A. A. MILNE

Pooh Invents a New Game

adapted by Stephen Krensky

with decorations by Ernest H. Shepard

Puffin Books

PUFFIN BOOKS
Published by the Penguin Group
Penguin Putnam Books for Young Readers, 345 Hudson Street, New York, New York 10014, U.S.A.
Penguin Books Ltd, 80 Strand, London WC2R ORL, England
Penguin Books Australia Ltd, 250 Camberwell Road, Camberwell, Victoria 3124, Australia
Penguin Books Canada Ltd, 10 Alcorn Avenue, Toronto, Ontario, Canada M4V 3B2
Penguin Books (N.Z.) Ltd, 182-190 Wairau Road, Auckland 10, New Zealand

Penguin Books Ltd, Registered Offices: Harmondsworth, Middlesex, England

Simultaneously published in the United States of America by Puffin Books and Dutton Children's Books,
divisions of Penguin Putnam Books for Young Readers, 2003

1 3 5 7 9 10 8 6 4 2

Puffin Easy-to-Read ISBN 0-14-250008-9
Puffin® and Easy-to-Read® are registered trademarks of Penguin Putnam Inc.

Printed in China.

Reading Level 2.2

CONTENTS

1

POOH HAS A MOVING EXPERIENCE

One day Winnie-the-Pooh

was walking through the Forest

toward a wooden bridge.

He was trying to make up

a piece of poetry about

fir-cones.

He picked up a fir-cone

and looked at it.

"This is a very good fir-cone,"

Pooh said to himself,

"and something ought

to rhyme with it."

But he couldn't think of anything.

And then this came into his head suddenly:

Here is a myst'ry

About a little fir-tree.

Owl says it's his tree,

And Kanga says it's her tree.

"Which doesn't make sense," said Pooh,

"because Kanga doesn't live in a tree."

He had just come to the bridge

and was not looking where

he was going.

Then he tripped over something,

and the fir-cone jerked out

of his paw into the river.

"Bother," said Pooh as it

floated under the bridge.

He looked at the river

as it slipped slowly away beneath him…

and suddenly, there was his fir-cone

slipping away too.

"That's funny," said Pooh.

"I dropped it on the other side,

and it came out on this side!

I wonder if it would do it again?"

And he went back for more fir-cones.

It did. It kept on doing it.

Then he dropped two in at once,

and leaned over the bridge

to see which of them

would come out first.

And one of them did.

But as they were both the same size,

Pooh didn't know if it was the one

that he wanted to win, or the other one.

So the next time he dropped in

one big one and one little one.

The big one came out first,

which was what he had said

it would do.

And the little one came out last,

which was what he had said

it would do.

So he had won twice.

And when he went home for tea,

he had won thirty-six and lost

twenty-eight, which meant

that he was—

well, you take twenty-eight from

thirty-six, and *that's* what he was.

Instead of the other way around.

2

EEYORE APPEARS UNEXPECTEDLY

That was the beginning

of the game called Poohsticks,

which Pooh invented.

He and his friends used to play it

on the edge of the Forest.

But they played with sticks

instead of fir-cones

because sticks were easier to mark.

Now one day Pooh and Piglet

and Rabbit and Roo

were all playing Poohsticks together.

They had dropped their sticks in

when Rabbit said "Go!"

Then they had hurried across

to the other side of the bridge,

and now they were all leaning

over the edge,

waiting to see whose stick

would come out first.

But it was a long time coming,

because the river was lazy that day,

and hardly seemed to mind

if it didn't ever get there at all.

"I can see mine!" cried Roo.

"No, I can't, it's something else.

Can you see yours, Piglet?

I thought I could see mine,

but I couldn't.

There it is!

No, it isn't.

Can you see yours, Pooh?"

"No," said Pooh.

"I expect my stick's stuck," said Roo.

"Rabbit, my stick's stuck.

Is your stick stuck, Piglet?"

"They always take longer

than you think," said Rabbit.

"How long do you *think* they'll take?"

asked Roo.

"I can see yours, Piglet,"

said Pooh suddenly.

"Mine's a sort of grayish one,"

said Piglet,

not daring to lean too far over

in case he fell in.

"Yes, that's what I can see.

It's coming over to my side."

Rabbit leaned over further than ever,

looking for his stick.

And Roo wriggled up and down,

calling out, "Come on, stick!

Stick, stick, stick!"

And Piglet got very excited

because his was the only one

which had been seen.

That meant he was winning.

"It's coming!" said Pooh.

"Are you *sure* it's mine?"

squeaked Piglet.

"Yes, because it's gray.

A big gray one.

Here it comes! A very—

big—gray—

Oh, no, it isn't, it's Eeyore."

And out floated Eeyore.

"Eeyore!" cried everybody.

Looking very calm,

very dignified,

with his legs in the air,

Eeyore came out from

beneath the bridge.

"It's Eeyore!" cried Roo,

terribly excited.

"Is that so?" said Eeyore,

getting caught up by a little eddy,

and turning around three times.

"I didn't know you were playing,"

said Roo.

"I'm not," said Eeyore.

"Eeyore, what *are* you doing there?"

said Rabbit.

"I'll give you three guesses, Rabbit.

Digging holes in the ground?

Wrong.

Leaping from branch to branch

of an oak-tree?

Wrong.

Waiting for somebody to help me

out of the river?

Right."

3

POOH GETS
AN IDEA

"But, Eeyore," said Pooh in distress,

"what can we—I mean, how shall

we—do you think if we——"

"Yes," said Eeyore.

"One of those would be

just the thing.

Thank you, Pooh."

"He's going *round* and *round*,"

said Roo, much impressed.

There was a moment's silence

while everybody thought.

"I've got a sort of idea,"

said Pooh at last.

"If we all threw stones and things into

the river on *one* side of Eeyore,

the stones would make waves,

and the waves would wash him

to the other side."

"That's a very good idea, Pooh,"

said Rabbit.

"Supposing we hit him by mistake?"

said Piglet anxiously.

"Or supposing you missed him

by mistake," said Eeyore.

But Pooh had got the biggest

stone he could carry,

and was leaning over the bridge,

holding it in his paws.

"I'm not throwing it,

I'm dropping it, Eeyore,"

he explained.

"And then I can't miss—

I mean I can't hit you.

Could you stop turning round

for a moment,

because it muddles me rather?"

"Now, Pooh," said Rabbit,

"when I say 'Now!'

you can drop it.

Piglet, give Pooh

a little more room.

Get back a bit there, Roo.

Are you ready?"

"No," said Eeyore.

"Now!" said Rabbit.

Pooh dropped his stone.

There was a loud splash,

and Eeyore disappeared....

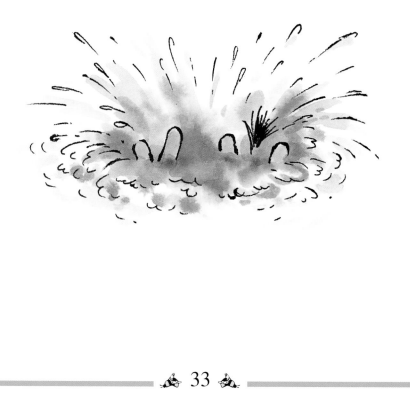

It was an anxious moment

for the watchers

on the bridge.

They looked and looked....

And even the sight

of Piglet's stick

coming out a little in front of Rabbit's

didn't cheer them up as much

as you would have expected.

And then something gray

showed for a moment

by the river bank…

and it got slowly bigger and bigger…

and at last Eeyore was coming out.

With a shout

everyone rushed off the bridge,

pushing and pulling at Eeyore.

And soon he was standing among

them again on dry land.

"Well done, Pooh," said Rabbit kindly.

"That was a good idea of ours.

But how did you fall in, Eeyore?"

"I didn't," said Eeyore.

"I was BOUNCED."

"Oo," said Roo excitedly.

"Did somebody push you?"

"Somebody BOUNCED me.

I was just thinking by the side

of the river—when I received

a very loud BOUNCE."

"Oh, Eeyore!" said everybody.

"Who did it?" asked Roo.

Eeyore didn't answer.

"I expect it was Tigger,"

said Piglet nervously.

"But Eeyore," said Pooh,

"was it a Joke or an Accident?

I mean—"

"I didn't stop to ask, Pooh.

I just floated to the surface,

and said to myself, 'It's wet.'"

"And where was Tigger?"

asked Rabbit.

4

CHRISTOPHER ROBIN SETTLES THINGS

Before Eeyore could answer,

there was a loud noise behind them.

Then through the hedge

came Tigger himself.

"Hallo, everybody,"

said Tigger cheerfully.

"Hallo, Tigger," said Roo.

"Tigger," Rabbit said solemnly,

"what happened just now?"

"Just when?" said Tigger

a little uncomfortably.

"When you bounced Eeyore

into the river."

"I didn't bounce him."

"You bounced me,"

said Eeyore gruffly.

"I didn't really.

I had a cough,

and I happened to be behind Eeyore.

'Grrrr—oppp—ptschschschz,' I said."

"That's what I call bouncing,"

said Eeyore.

"Very unpleasant habit.

I don't mind Tigger being in the Forest.

It's a large Forest,

and there's plenty of room to

bounce in it."

"But I don't see why he should come

into *my* little corner of it,

and bounce there."

"I didn't bounce, I coughed,"

said Tigger crossly.

"Bouncy or coffy," said Eeyore,

"it's all the same at the bottom

of the river."

"Well," said Rabbit,

"all I can say is—

well, here's Christopher Robin,

so *he* can say it."

Christopher Robin had come down

from the Forest to the bridge,

feeling all sunny and careless.

But when he saw all the animals there,

he knew it wasn't that kind of afternoon.

"It's like this," said Rabbit. "Tigger—"

"No, I didn't," said Tigger.

"Well, anyhow, there I was,"

   said Eeyore.

"But I don't think he meant to,"

   said Pooh.

"He just *is* bouncy," said Piglet,

"and he can't help it."

"Try bouncing *me,* Tigger,"

said Roo eagerly.

"Eeyore, Tigger's going to try *me.*"

"Yes, yes," said Rabbit,

"we don't all want to speak at once.

The point is, what does

Christopher Robin think?"

"All I did was cough," said Tigger.

"He bounced," said Eeyore.

"Well, I sort of boffed," said Tigger.

"Hush!" said Rabbit,

holding up his paw.

"What do you say, Christopher Robin?"

"Well," said Christopher Robin,

not quite sure what it was all about,

"*I* think—"

"Yes?" said everybody.

"*I* think we all ought to play

Poohsticks."

So they did.

And Eeyore,

who had never played it before,

won more times than anybody else.